A First-Start® Easy Reader

This easy reader contains only 36 different words,
repeated often to help the young reader develop
word recognition and interest in reading.

Basic word list for *Rub-a-Dub Suds*

a	love	scrubs
and	loves	she
bath	more	some
dub	need	suds
full	of	take
get	plug	Tammy
harder	pull	the
higher	pulls	to
I	puts	tub
in	rub	water
is	rubs	where
lots	scrub	with

Rub-a-Dub Suds

Written by Sharon Peters

Illustrated by Penny Carter

Troll Associates

Library of Congress Cataloging in Publication Data

Peters, Sharon.
   Rub-a-dub suds.

   Summary: Tammy the pig loves to take a bath and
fills the tub with more and more suds.
   [1. Baths—Fiction. 2. Pigs—Fiction]
I. Carter, Penny, ill. II. Title.
PZ7.P44183Ru   1987   [E]   86-30856
ISBN 0-8167-0984-X (lib. bdg.)
ISBN 0-8167-0985-8 (pbk.)

Copyright © 1988 by Troll Associates

10 9 8 7 6 5 4 3

Tammy loves a bath.

She loves to take a bath.

Tammy loves lots of suds.

She loves a tub full of suds.

Tammy puts in the plug.

Tammy puts in the suds.

She puts in some water.

"Rub-a-dub."

"I need some more suds."

Tammy puts in more suds.

She puts in more water.

"Rub-a-dub.

I love to scrub with suds."

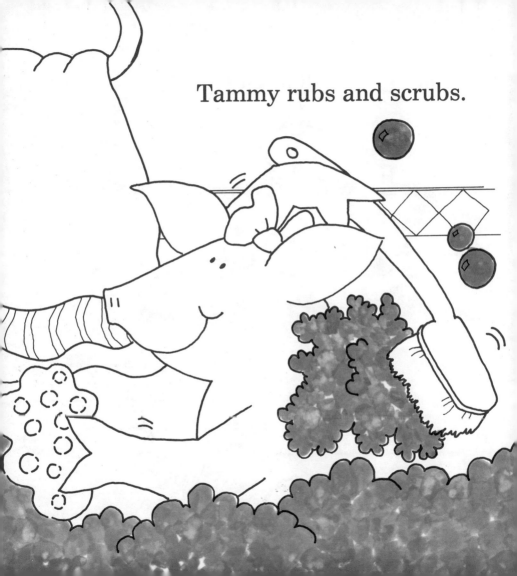

Tammy rubs and scrubs.

The tub is full of suds.

Tammy scrubs harder and harder.

The suds get higher and higher.

Tammy puts in more suds.

Tammy scrubs and rubs.

The suds get higher and higher.

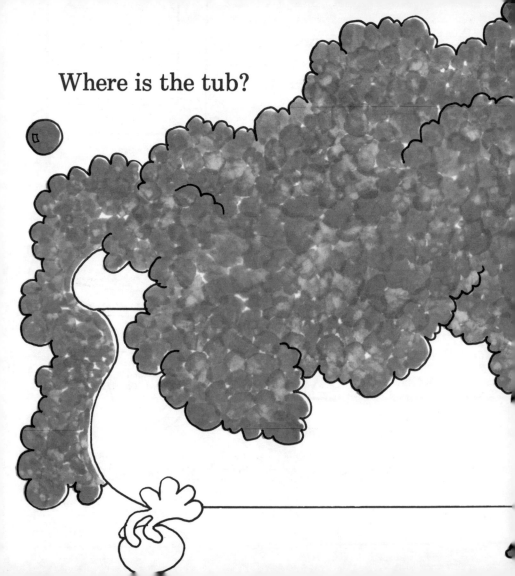

Where is the tub?

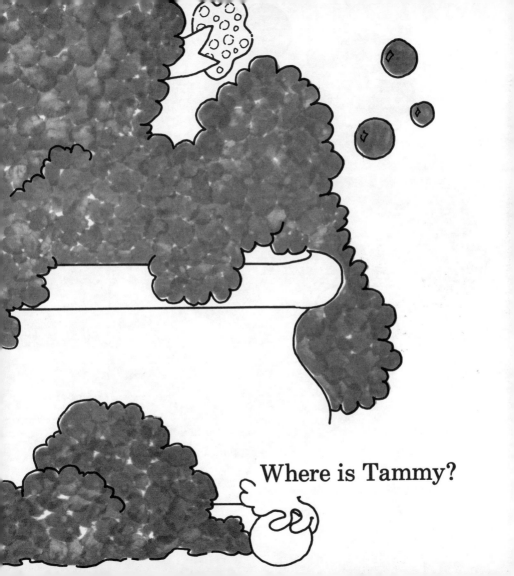

Where is Tammy?

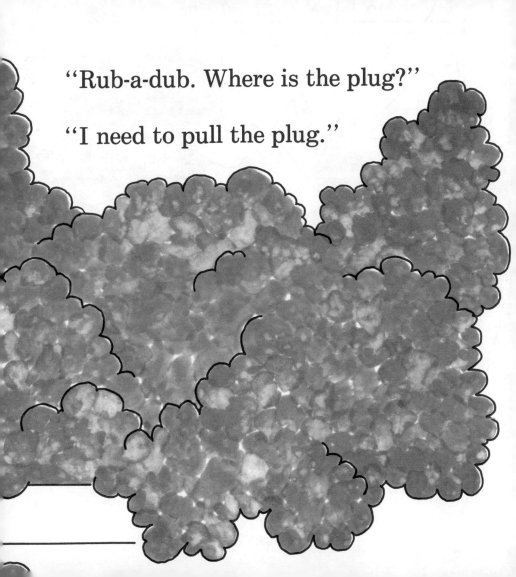

"Rub-a-dub. Where is the plug?"

"I need to pull the plug."

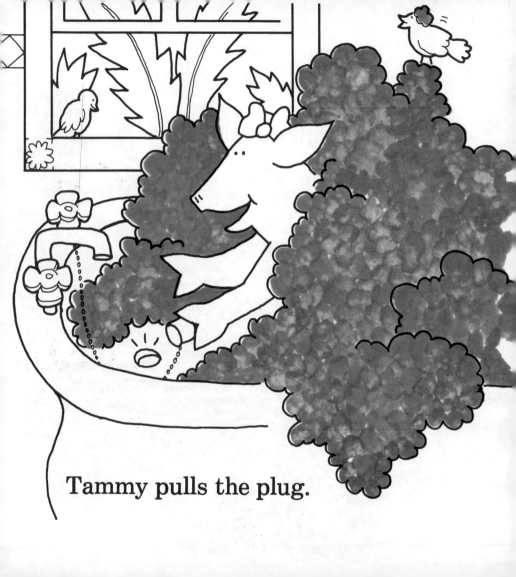

Tammy pulls the plug.

"Rub-a-dub. I love suds!"